Date: 11/8/21

J 636.93592 BAN
Bankston, John,
Caring for my new guinea pig

HOW TO CARE FOR YOUR NEW PET

CARING FOR
MY NEW
GUINEA PIG

John Bankston

Mitchell Lane

PUBLISHERS

2001 SW 31st Avenue
Hallandale, FL 33009
www.mitchelllane.com

First Edition, 2021.

Author: John Bankston
Designer: Ed Morgan
Editor: Morgan Brody

Names/credits:
Title: Caring for My New Guinea Pig / by John Bankston
Description: Hallandale, FL : Mitchell Lane Publishers

Series: How to Care for Your New Pet

Library bound ISBN: 978-1-58415-158-6

eBook ISBN: 978-1-58415-159-3

Photo credits: Freepik.com, Shutterstock

CONTENTS

Words in **bold**
throughout can be
found in the Glossary.

Guinea Pig History

Over 400 years ago, Spanish explorers returned home with a special gift. Incas had given them guinea pigs! In Europe, they became popular as pets. Guinea pigs are still a favorite pet.

Guinea pigs make great pets. They rarely bite. They are friendly and love people. No pet is perfect. Guinea pigs only sleep four hours a day. That means they are awake at night. They get noisy. If you have a messy room, you'll relate to guinea pigs. They like messy cages. You'll be very busy keeping your room and their cage clean. Learn about their **habits** before you bring one home.

DID YOU KNOW?

Some people think Guinea pigs got their name from the squealing sounds they make.

Guinea Pig Facts

Guinea pigs aren't from Guinea in West Africa. They come from South American countries like Ecuador, Bolivia, and Peru. They are related to the cavy (kay-vee). A cavy is another name for guinea pigs.

They aren't pigs either. They are rodents. Gerbils, hamsters, and mice are all rodents. A rodent's strong teeth never stop growing. They need to gnaw on something hard. Beavers are the biggest rodents in North America.

Guinea pigs can grow to almost two feet long and weigh around two pounds. Most are like the American Guinea Pig with short, smooth fur. The Texel has long, curly hair. The White Crested is named for the spot on its forehead. An adult Peruvian's fur grows over its face. Coats can be black, white, brown or a mix.

Like pigs, they are chubby with nubby tails and thick necks. They even snort or grunt. Guinea pigs also whistle. They do this when they want to be held. If they hear you getting food, they will whistle for a treat.

DID YOU KNOW?

A young guinea pig can run when they are only three hours old.

Get Ready for a Guinea Pig

You want your new pet to be happy. Do this by getting its home ready. Have an adult help. Your room may not be best because the sounds guinea pigs make during the night may keep you awake. Their cages require enough space for them to be active.

Guinea pigs don't do well in the cold. They also hate the heat. This is because they can't sweat. Sweating helps other animals and humans cool off on a hot day. When it is too warm, guinea pigs can get sick. Find a space that is around 75 degrees Fahrenheit.

Make a space safe by removing plants they can reach or cords they can chew. An adult can help find plastic covers for the cords. Electric cords are very dangerous because guineas like to chew on them.

Their new home shouldn't be near a heating vent or a fireplace. Avoid cold garages. Don't put their home near a window or doorway. A damp bathroom is a bad idea because mold can grow on their bedding.

Guinea pigs have great hearing. But they don't see very well. Don't ever put them on a table or desk when they are out of their cage. It's too easy for them to fall. They have delicate spines that can be injured. This is also why you want to be gentle with them. The floor is a great spot for their cage. After choosing the right space, it's time to go shopping!

Guinea Pig Habitat

Guinea pigs live up to their name. They are big! Don't get a guinea pig cage made for gerbils or hamsters. Guinea pigs don't like climbing. They exercise on the floor of the cage.

A guinea pig's home is called a **habitat**. In the wild, a guinea pig's habitat is underground in **burrows**.

If you are thinking of getting a guinea pig, try to get its cage ready before you bring it home. You will probably bring your new pet home in a critter **carrier** of some sort. It may be a little uncomfortable for your guinea pig to stay in it for any length of time. So, having its cage prepared will help to make your new pet feel happy in its new home.

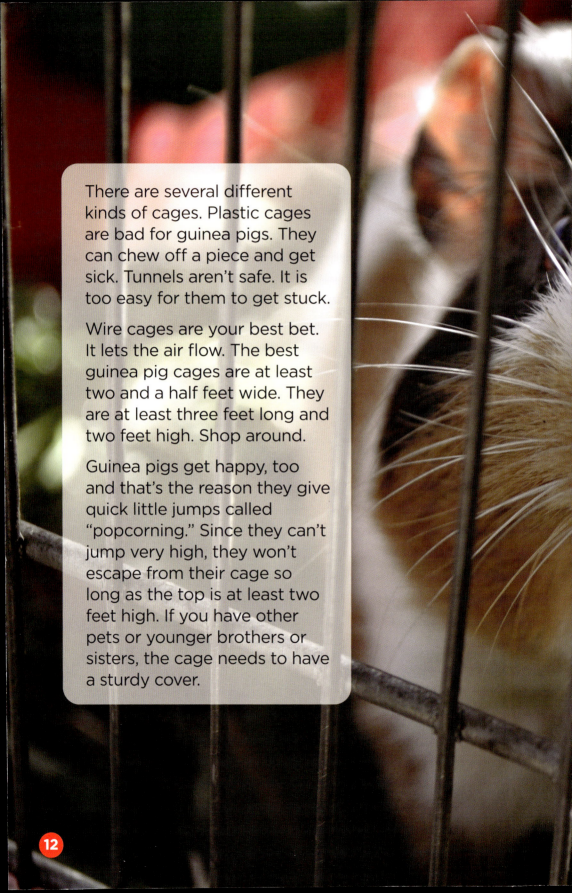

There are several different kinds of cages. Plastic cages are bad for guinea pigs. They can chew off a piece and get sick. Tunnels aren't safe. It is too easy for them to get stuck.

Wire cages are your best bet. It lets the air flow. The best guinea pig cages are at least two and a half feet wide. They are at least three feet long and two feet high. Shop around.

Guinea pigs get happy, too and that's the reason they give quick little jumps called "popcorning." Since they can't jump very high, they won't escape from their cage so long as the top is at least two feet high. If you have other pets or younger brothers or sisters, the cage needs to have a sturdy cover.

Some guinea pig cages connect. That makes expanding their home easier. Dividers make it easy to put the guinea pig on one side while you clean the other. If you have two guinea pigs, two connected cages are perfect. They can cuddle. But they also have their own space.

Metal wire hurts guinea pig's feet. Just like you, they need a floor. Use a mat over the bottom of the cage. Find some paper without ink and tear it into strips. Don't use magazines or newspapers. Cover the mat with two inches of shredded paper. Add another few inches of deep straw or hay on top of the paper. This will give your guinea pig a comfy place to sleep.

Don't use cedar or pine shavings. They can make guinea pigs sick.

Also do *not* put an exercise wheel in the cage. Guinea pigs can hurt their back or feet on them.

Food can be
put in a small dish
that doesn't tip over
easily. Use ceramic, *not*
metal or plastic bowls.

Hang a bottle on the side of the
cage. There are special ones made
to hold your guinea pig's water. Buy
one that is made of metal or glass. Do not
use plastic. Make sure it is low enough for
your guinea to reach but high enough that it
doesn't make his bed all soggy.

On the other side, make a bed from a small
cardboard box. Use torn paper towels or tissues for
bedding. These should be plain and white.

Wild guinea pigs hide to stay safe. Your new friend will
hide for fun. Have an adult help you cut openings in a
small box. You can buy a large pipe. Make sure it is big
enough, so your guinea pig doesn't get stuck. Pet
shops sell wooden houses for small pets. Your new
friend will also enjoy chewing their home.

DID YOU KNOW?

Guinea pigs have four toes on their front
feet but only three on their hind feet.

Getting Your Piggy

Have you heard about dog shows? Purebred dogs like German Shepherds and Chihuahuas compete for "Best in Show." There are guinea pig shows, too!

Guinea pigs usually cost less than $50 at your local pet store. Pet stores also sell cages and other **paraphernalia** to make your pet's new home a fun place to live.

Your local shelter offers more than dogs and cats. They might have guinea pigs. Shelters check for illnesses. They often have supplies including cages and food. **Adopting** is a great way to find your new friend!

If you want to show your cavy or piggy at "Best in Show" or just want an unusual type, breeders can help. There are 13 **breeds** of guinea pigs. Buying from a breeder can cost more. But you may get to meet your guinea pig's mom and dad. Guinea pig babies need lots of care and love.

Pick up your guinea pig by holding it near the shoulders with one hand. Support its back with the other. The breeder can help show you how to hold your piggy. It should be calm once it gets to know you.

Check its fur and skin. The fur should be fluffy. It should not have bald spots. The skin shouldn't have lumps. Its eyes should be clear and bright. It should have energy. A healthy pig is a happy pig.

DID YOU KNOW?

Just like pigs, male guineas are called boars. Females are sows.

Happy Pigs

What makes a guinea pig happy? One way to keep them happy is to take good care of them. It's very important to keep their cage clean. Even if you beg, they will not clean their cage. It's your job.

Every day remove any dirty paper. Once a week put your guinea pig in its critter keeper or a closed off section of the cage. Then remove all the paper. Use a pet-safe cleaning product (an adult can help you find one).

You will also see large, sticky pellets. Leave these in the cage. They are called *caecotrophs*. Eating them helps your guinea pig stay healthy.

Clean their food dish and water bottle every day. Avoid lemon scented dish soap.

Guinea pigs are cuddly and full of personality. Unlike dogs and cats, guinea pigs typically need minimal **grooming** and are fairly simple to care for. Grooming includes nail trimming, coat brushing, and occasional bathing. Most guinea pig owners find that with a little training, they can learn to groom their pets at home.

Guinea pigs like to play with paper bags and cardboard boxes. They also like cat and rabbit toys. Only use hard toys that they cannot chew into bits.

Guinea pigs are **social**. They like to be in groups. Spending time with your guinea will help keep it happy. You may also want to get another guinea pig. Two boys or two girls are best.

Getting Piggy with It!

You will never have to ask your guinea pig to eat its vegetables. That's because guinea pigs are **vegetarians**. This means they don't eat meat. Hay is not just for horses. It's for guinea pigs, too! Hay should be their main meal. It not only fills them up, it helps keep their teeth from getting too long.

Remember to keep their water fresh. Guinea pigs drink a lot of water. Make sure they have all they need.

You can also give them a small spoonful of pellets. Sweet-smelling, green hay helps keep their bones and teeth healthy. Vitamin C is also important.

People can get Vitamin C from oranges. Broccoli and red peppers are better for guinea pigs. Have an adult help you slice up the veggies. Make sure you rinse them before you give them to your guinea pig.

Fruit has too much sugar for your new pet. Only give fruit once a week or so as a treat. It's like candy for guinea pigs!

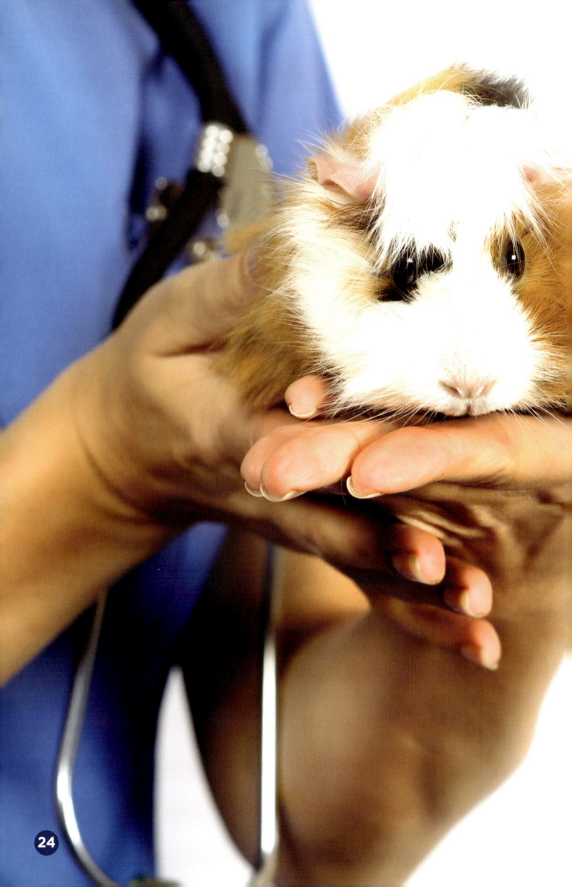

Going to the Vet

Guinea pigs are like people. They need check-ups once a year. Doctors for animals are called **veterinarians**. Don't wait until your new friend is sick. Take it to the vet the week you bring it home unless the vet at the shelter has examined it.

Vets will look at the guinea pig's teeth. Overgrown teeth are painful and can make your guinea pig sick. The vet will also make sure it doesn't have lice or mites and that its bones are healthy.

Exercise keeps your guinea pig healthy. So does a bit of sun. Wild guinea pigs get lots of sunshine. This helps it make Vitamin D.

A yard or balcony is perfect. Keep your guinea in a cage or enclosure even when they are outside. Don't leave it alone. Remember birds and larger animals can be dangerous. Also don't spend too long outside. Guinea pigs can get hot quickly.

Outside you can use a wire pen made for a small dog. But lots of guinea pig owners use kiddie pools. This is the perfect play space. You can even use it inside. Just don't fill it with water! Your piggy would rather "swim" in hay.

Give your guinea pig lots of playtime. Take care of its health and keep the cage clean. If you do this, the two of you will have many wonderful years together.

SHOPPING LIST

When you are ready to bring home your guinea pig, have an adult take you to your local pet store. This is a list of some things you will need:

- ☐ Large cage or modular enclosure

- ☐ Bedding material

- ☐ Hidey box

- ☐ Food dish

- ☐ Water bottle (a drip bottle that can be hung on the side of the cage)

- ☐ High-quality pellets

- ☐ Timothy hay

- ☐ Fresh Vegetables

- ☐ Treats

- ☐ Toys

- ☐ Grooming tools

- ☐ A critter-keeper to bring it home

FIND OUT MORE

Online

There are several sites that will help you raise a healthy and happy guinea pig:

The Humane Society offers advice and can help you find shelters where you can adopt your guinea pig:

https://www.humanesociety.org/resources/guinea-pigs-right-pet-you

https://www.humanesociety.org/resources/guinea-pig-housing

The American Cavy Breeders Association has a full list of registered guinea pig breeders in the United States. Your local cavy club will also be able to recommend a good local breeder.

http://www.acbaonline.com/index.html

"Fun Guinea Pig Facts," VetBabble. January 29, 2019

https://www.vetbabble.com/small-pets/fun-guinea-pig-facts/

Petfinder connects people with adoptable animals. They even have a section for "small and furry" animals like guinea pigs.

https://www.petfinder.com/search/small-furry-for-adoption/us

Learn all about the different noises your guinea pig makes:

http://youtu.be/BB8j3X3UyZA

Books

Marsico, Katie. *Guinea Pigs.* New York: Children's Press. 2015.

Vanderlip, Sharon Lynn. *The Guinea Pig Handbook*. Hauppauge, N.Y.: Barron's, 2015.

GLOSSARY

adopting
Taking care of someone without a family

breeds
Specific type of animal

burrow
Hole dug by a small animal

carrier
Safe container to transport an animal

grooming
To clean and care for an animal

habits
Regular behavior

habitat
Natural home of an animal

paraphernalia
Objects that are used to do a particular activity

social
Comfortable playing and being around others

vegetarians
Doesn't eat meat

veterinarian
Doctor who specializes in animal care

BIBLIOGRAPHY

"American Cavy Breeders Association." http://www.acbaonline.com/index.html

Dell' Amore, Christine. "Guinea Pigs Were Widespread as Elizabethan Pets." *National Geographic*. February 9, 2012. https://news.nationalgeographic. com/news/2012/01/120207-guinea-pigs-europe-south-america-pets-animals/

Graham, Sarah. "Giant Extinct Rodent Was Guinea Pig Relative." on September 19, 2003. https://www.scientificamerican.com/article/giant-extinct-rodent-was/

"Guinea Pig Trivia, Facts, and Care Tips." *VetBabble*. December 3, 2018. https://www.vetbabble.com/small-pets/guinea-pigs/guinea-pig-care-guide/

Sandlin, Amanda. "Leaping Guinea Pig." *National Geographic Kids*. February 2017.

McLeod, DVM. Lianne. "Cages for Guinea Pigs: Setting up a Guinea Pig Home." *The Spruce Pets*. December 15, 2018. https://www.thesprucepets. com/cages-for-guinea-pigs-1236839

Nefer, Barbara. "Kiddie Pools Make Great Guinea Pig Playpens." *The Spruce Pets*. April 2, 2019. https://www.thesprucepets.com/swimming-pool-as-guinea-pig-playpen-2662172

Quesenberry, DVM, MPH, DABVP (Avian). Katherine E. "Introduction to Guinea Pigs." MSD Vet Manual. https://www.msdvetmanual.com/all-other-pets/guinea-pigs/introduction-to-guinea-pigs

INDEX

ABOUT THE AUTHOR

John Bankston

The author of over 100 books for young readers, John Bankston lives in Miami Beach, Florida with his rescue dog Astronaut. He enjoys writing about a variety of pets and the ways people can help them thrive.